BOYS VS. GIRLS

by Erica David

Illustrated by Artful Doodlers

SCHOLASTIC INC.

New York   Toronto   London   Auckland   Sydney
Mexico City   New Delhi   Hong Kong   Buenos Aires

Published by Scholastic Inc.,
90 Old Sherman Turnpike, Danbury, Connecticut 06816.

SCHOLASTIC and associated logos are trademarks
and/or registered trademarks of Scholastic Inc.

ISBN 0-439-78279-1

First Scholastic Printing, September 2005

CHAPTERS

CHAPTER 1

THE ASSIGNMENT

"In honor of school spirit week, I'm giving you all a special assignment," Mrs. Keats, the English teacher announced. "You'll each research an important person in the history of the school."

MELVIN SPARKLE
DANNY COOLIDGE
KEVIN BAKER
JAMES WAKE

Kimi Finster looked at the names of the research subjects listed on the board. "Is it just me," she whispered to her friend Lil Deville, "or are they all men?"

"They're men all right," Lil whispered back.

"Like women had nothing to do with the history of this school," Kimi muttered. She slammed her notebook shut in a huff.

After class, Kimi was still fuming about the assignment.

"I don't see why you're so mad," said Lil's brother Phil Deville.

"You wouldn't, Philip," Lil snapped.

"Think about it. We're always researching men," Kimi explained. "It's as if women aren't important enough to be paper topics!"

"Well, maybe they aren't," Phil offered, with a shrug.

"Of course, they are!" Lil cried. "Everyone knows that girls are superior!"

"I wouldn't say that," Chuckie Finster spoke up.

"What do you mean?" Kimi asked, frostily.

"I'm just saying that boys and girls are equal," answered Chuckie.

"How could you?" Lil shouted.

"What? What did I say?" Chuckie asked, confused.

"You think that girls can't do better than boys!" Kimi accused.

"I didn't say that!" Chuckie exclaimed.

"Well, we'll see about that," Kimi said. "Come on, Lil."

Later that day, Phil and Chuckie met their friend Tommy Pickles at the school track.

"I can't wait for the big spirit week relay race," said Phil. "We're gonna win this year for sure!"

"Not if we don't practice," Chuckie said.

"And we can't practice without Kimi,"
Tommy added. "Where is she?"

"Uh, I don't think she's coming,"
Phil mumbled.

"Why not?" Tommy asked.

"Chuckie made her mad," answered Phil.

"Me?" Chuckie cried. "I'm not the one who said girls weren't important!"

"What did you say that for, Phil?" asked Tommy.

"'Cause girls are weird, Tommy," Phil replied. "They don't like burping or armpit noises. They're no fun."

"I dunno, Phil," Chuckie said. "Some of them smell kinda nice."

Just then Kimi walked over to meet the boys with Lil close behind.

"Kimi, I'm glad you came," Tommy greeted her.

"I'm not staying," Kimi snapped. "I just came by to tell you that I'm quitting the relay team."

"But you can't quit, the race is in four days!" Tommy pleaded.

"Well, I guess you'll have to find someone else," said Kimi. "And since girls aren't important, I hope it's a boy."

"If that's the way it's gotta be," Phil replied coolly.

"FYI, Philip. Kimi and I are starting our own relay team. Girls only," Lil explained. "And we're going to leave you in the dust."

With that, Kimi and Lil linked arms and walked off.

"Way to go, Phil," Tommy muttered.

"Yeah, nice goin', Chuckie," Phil

mumbled, passing the blame.

"It isn't my fault!" Chuckie wailed.

The next afternoon, Kimi and Chuckie waited on customers at the Java Lava coffee shop.

"I'll have one pineapple-banana super smoothie," the next person in line said.

"I've got it!" Chuckie called, grabbing a pineapple.

"No, I've got it!" Kimi said. She snatched the pineapple from Chuckie and hurried over to the blenders.

"No fair," Chuckie complained. "That's my customer."

"Oh, so you think I can't make a smoothie as well as you can?" Kimi asked.

Chuckie argued, "I never said—"

"You think that because I'm a girl, I'm incapable of using a blender?!" Kimi roared. "Girls rule, Chuckie, and I'm going to prove it."

She picked up another pineapple and tossed it to her brother. "Whoever makes the fastest smoothie wins," she announced.

"You're on," Chuckie said.

On the count of three, Kimi and Chuckie leaped into action. Kimi gave her brother a smug grin as she quickly chopped her fruit.

Chuckie smirked back at her. He had a
plan. He shoved the whole pineapple into
his blender to save time.

Unfortunately, Chuckie's plan backfired. When he switched on his blender, it lurched and sputtered. Suddenly it erupted sending chunks of pineapple sailing into the air.

Pineapple chunks hit Kimi in the head just as she was pouring her smoothie into a cup. She ducked and knocked her cup over, spilling smoothie everywhere.

"You klutz!" Kimi hissed.

"Klutz? I'm not the one who knocked her cup over!" shouted Chuckie.

"Excuse me," the customer interrupted. "I ordered a smoothie, not a circus act."

"Ma'am," Kimi began, "I—"

"I guess I'll go to that other shop down the street," the customer snapped. She walked out of the store, leaving Kimi and Chuckie glaring at each other.

The following day, Phil went to the video arcade after school. His sister Lil was already there playing one of their favorite video games, Alien Invasion.

"Move over, Lil," Phil said. "Let me show you how it's done."

"Why would I need help from a boy?" Lil asked. "I'm perfectly capable of stopping the alien invasion on my own."

"I think you're forgetting that I hold the high score for this game," Phil bragged.

"Not anymore," Lil said, snidely. She pointed to her name now at the top of the high score list.

"But that's impossible!" Phil cried.

"Why? Because I'm a girl?" asked Lil.

"Outta my way, Lillian!" Phil shouted.

Before Lil could start another game, Phil slid in front of the controls and dropped in a token. "I'm gonna get my high score back if it's the last thing I do!" he declared.

"Don't hold your breath," Lil quipped, as she stomped away.

Phil played game after game of Alien Invasion, but the best he could do was tie Lil's high score. When the arcade owner kicked him out at closing, Phil realized he had missed dinner, spent all of his money, and was probably in deep trouble for not calling home.

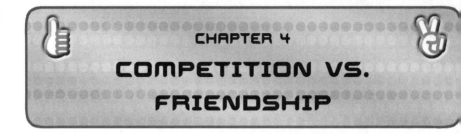

CHAPTER 4
COMPETITION VS. FRIENDSHIP

The day before the race, Tommy, Chuckie and Phil sat in a booth at the Java Lava.

"Hey, why the long faces?" asked Phil's mom, Betty Deville.

"The girls are mad at us," Chuckie mumbled.

"Why? What did you do?" Betty said.

"What did I do?" Chuckie cried. "Why is it always *my* fault?"

"Somehow everything's turned into boys vs. girls," Tommy explained.

"That's not so bad," Betty said. "A little competition is healthy."

"It doesn't feel healthy," Chuckie muttered. "Ever since the smoothie showdown, Kimi won't speak to me."

"Sounds like the competition is getting in the way of your friendship," Betty observed.

"We don't have time for friendship!" Phil declared. "We gotta prove we're better by winning that race tomorrow."

"So let me see if I have this right," Betty said. "Proving you're better than someone is more important than being friends with her?"

"If by someone you mean my sister, then yes," Phil replied.

"I see. You boys have a lot to learn!"

Betty turned her back and walked away.

"Great, now your mom's mad at us!"
Chuckie moaned.

"Women!" Phil muttered in exasperation.

It was the day of the relay race and all of the students gathered at the school track to participate.

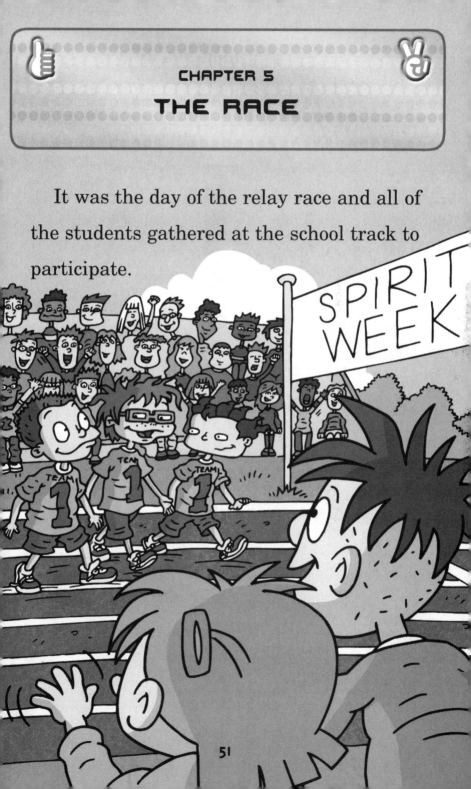

Tommy, Phil, Chuckie, and Dil lined
up with the other teams.

Kimi, Lil, Angelica, and Susie stood
beside them at the starting line.

"You look worried, Philip. Are you afraid a girl might beat you?" Lil asked.

"Not gonna happen," Phil replied.

The race began with Dil and Susie running the first lap. Susie took the lead and was the first to hand her baton off to Angelica.

As Angelica ran down the track, she noticed Tommy behind her.

"You're toast, Pickles!" she taunted.

"Don't count on it," Tommy replied. He sped up, passing Angelica and several other students to hand the baton to Chuckie.

Chuckie took off in the lead, but Kimi quickly caught up with him. "See ya, Chuckie," she teased, as she swept past.

The race continued with Phil and Lil sprinting into the home stretch.

"Prepare to lose, Philip," cried Lil.

"Never!" Phil huffed. But before either of them could cross the finish line, a boy from another team surged ahead and won.

"No way!" Phil and Lil cried in unison.

Moments later everyone gathered
at the finish line.

"I don't get it!" Kimi exclaimed.
"We should have won."

"Instead, you got beat by a boy,"
Phil replied.

"So did you!" Lil snapped.

"No, look at the winning team," Tommy said. "It's made up of boys and girls."

"So, what's your point, Tommy?" asked Lil.

"I think Tommy's saying that we should've been working together," Kimi answered.

"Together? But what about our girl power?" Lil said.

"Girls still rule," Kimi responded. "But maybe boys rule, too, in their own weird way."

"Weird is right," Lil agreed, staring at her brother.

"You girls are the weird ones," Phil said. "I mean, how can you not like armpit noises?"